A Little Mom
of Kindness *for:*

. . . .

First published in Great Britain in 2018 by Hodder & Stoughton
An Hachette UK company

1

A CIP catalogue record for this title is available from the British Library

ISBN 978 1 473 69171 1
eBook ISBN 978 1 473 69172 8

Set in Baskerville by Anna Woodbine, thewoodbineworkshop.co.uk
Printed and bound in Italy by Lego S.p.A.

Hodder & Stoughton policy is to use papers that are natural, renewable and recyclable products and made from wood grown in sustainable forests. The logging and manufacturing processes are expected to conform to the environmental regulations of the country of origin.

Hodder & Stoughton Ltd
Carmelite House
50 Victoria Embankment
London EC4Y 0DZ

www.hodderfaith.com

Dear Parents

I have called these books Little Moments *(not* Vast Hours*!)*
because I want them to be just that. A moment to pause in you and
your child's busy day. A moment to step away from the hustle and
bustle of life. A moment simply to be still.

The Bible is full of the most amazing stories, written down by many
authors over hundreds of years, all of them inspired to share the story
of this wonderful God and his amazing love for his children.
The words in this book are not literal translations – they are inspired
by verses and passages that I love.

My hope for all my readers, big and small, is that the
words and pictures will connect you to the true heart of God
and that the truth of who God is and how much
God loves you will nestle deep in your heart.

Jenny

Take a moment to watch the birds fly.

They are full of freedom
and have no cares!
Are you not far more
precious to God
than them?

Matthew 6:26

Don't just love with your words but give comfort by the things that you do.

1 John 3:18

I am on the path of life!

God has filled me with the
joy of God's presence as
we travel together.

Psalm 16:11

I am not afraid
of being weak,
for then I know what it
is to be carried
by God's strength.

God is the one
who hides me
and protects me.
When I am
in trouble
God rushes to rescue me.

Psalm 46:1

Neither the sea,

nor the rivers will wash over me

because God will make a
safe path for me through
the middle.

Psalm 69:13-15

God is

like

a

strong

tower,

run into it and enjoy

being wrapped in safety.

Proverbs 18:10

When trouble comes,

God will comfort you...

...and you will then carry that comfort in your heart to give to others who are hurting.

2 Corinthians 1:3-4

You have given me

a hiding place where I can

s i n g

my heart out to you.

I wept alone,
but God heard me
and came close
so that I could give God
my requests.

Psalm 6:8-9

Above the rain clouds
there is always s u n s h i n e;
dance until the
sun breaks through.

Song of Songs 2:11

You have nothing to fear,
have courage!
God is with you and
you will go together.

God is the kindest shepherd,
gathering you in,
holding you close
to the beat of
God's heart,
and leading you gently
along the right path.

Isaiah 40:11

God has counted
every hair on your head!
That's how well
G o d   k n o w s   y o u .

Luke 12:7

God has prepared
a good path
for you to walk on,
leading you into
a future of hope.

Jeremiah 29:11

Lay down all your troubles
before God and only
carry with you the
love from God's
h e a r t.

God draws so near
to you when your heart
is broken and you cannot
take another step.

God has collected
my tears in a bottle,
not a single one has
been lost.

Psalm 56:8

Even when my path
is hidden in darkness I
have nothing to fear, for God
is walking with me,
moment by moment,
step by step.

Psalm 23:4

There may be sorrow
in the night but joy
b u r s t s
through in the morning.

Psalm 30:5

God heals the broken-hearted

and wraps up

their wounds

in bandages of love.

You have a friend
who
walks beside you,
closer than your breath
and nearer than your
hands and feet.

Proverbs 18:24

When you have lost
all hope your God will
turn your sorrow into a
garden bursting with life
and beauty and joy.

Isaiah 51:3

As a mother
draws her children close
to comfort them so
God comforts you.

Isaiah 66:13

Give comfort
to your friends and
build each other up,
then you will grow
s t r o n g
together.

1 Thessalonians 5:11

God will lift you

from your sorrow and

place you in safety.

Job 5:11

God feels our pain
and weeps with us
in our sorrow.

John 11:33-35

The day is done
and I *lay* my head to sleep
with God beside me,
covered with a
blanket of safety.

Psalm 4:8